Danny the Detective

and other stories

Written by
NICOLA BAXTER

Illustrated by
ANDREW WARRINGTON

This is a Parragon Book
This edition published in 2002

Parragon
Queen Street House
4 Queen Street
Bath BA1 1HE, UK

Copyright © Parragon 2000

ISBN 0-75259-495-8

Produced for Parragon by
Nicola Baxter

Designed by Amanda Hawkes
Cover designed by Gemma Hornsby
Cover illustrated by Andrew Everitt-Stewart
Additional illustrations by Richard Duszczak

Printed in Italy

Contents

Danny
the
Detective

Detectives have to be nosy. There are just no two ways about it. If you are not curious about *what* people do and *why* they do it, it is no good considering a career as a private eye.

Danny Dickson was determined to be a detective when he grew up. He thought is was probably best if he started now, while he was still young. He was pretty sure there were all sorts of skills that he could develop so that when he finally launched himself upon an unsuspecting world as Danny Dickson Investigations, he would quite simply be the best.

But Danny already had the biggest qualification for being a detective—he was the nosiest boy you ever met. And on one occasion at least, this was his downfall.

Danny had been watching old Mrs. Davies down the street for some time. Danny himself called it surveillance. Mrs. Davies called it spying. She was a woman who kept herself to herself. Not for her the morning gossip over the fence with her neighbours. She rarely had visitors and hardly ever went out. Danny had heard his parents talking about their shy neighbour. To his mind, her behaviour was far from normal. He decided, for no very good reason, that the reason she was so seldom seen out and about was that she had something to hide. He was determined to find out what it was.

As a matter of fact, Mrs. Davies was a great scholar. Her passion in life was

deciphering Egyptian hieroglyphics. She wasn't interested in people today very much at all, but she was very interested in people who lived over two thousand years ago. She spent day after day, and very often night after night, pouring over ancient texts.

It didn't occur to Danny Dickson that Mrs. Davies had better things to do than shopping and gossiping, but if it had, I'm afraid his behaviour would have been the same. He was simply curious by nature.

Once he decided to begin watching Mrs. Davies, Danny equipped himself in a methodical manner. He bought a new blue notebook and wrote on the front of it: "Subject X". He didn't think it was professional to use the subject's real name on what he called a "dossier". Next the boy-detective borrowed his father's best binoculars (Mr. Dickson was a keen bird-watcher) and tried out all the front-facing windows in his house to see which gave the best view of Mrs. Davies' front door. Luckily, the best window was in his own bedroom. Danny would be able to watch night and day if he wished. Finally, he went to the shops and bought himself a bag of surveillance provisions. Danny was a boy who liked his food and he found that long hours of watching could be even more tedious if he didn't have a bag of drinks and munchies close at hand.

At last, when everything was ready, Danny opened his new notebook on the first page and wrote, "Day 1: Thursday

1st September: 0800 hours" at the top. His long vigil had begun.

But Danny was about to have a very frustrating time. Although Mrs. Davies very rarely came out of her front door, she did have to get food and other necessities like anyone else. A couple of times a week, she set off with a little basket on wheels to buy what she needed.

But Mrs. Davies was a woman who had all her wits about her. The first time she left the house after Danny's regime had begun, she looked up and noticed a boy staring at her through partly-drawn curtains. It was odd, but she thought no more about it.

Later, when she returned from her shopping, Mrs. Davies happened to look up again. The boy was still there. Hmm.

It didn't take Mrs. Davies long to realize that it wasn't only when she went

out that the boy peered out from behind his curtains. She did a bit of peering out herself and saw that he sat, hardly moving except to reach into a bag by his side, hour after hour and stared at her house.

Mrs. Davies felt a little disturbed. It wasn't, she felt, natural for a boy of any age to be sitting still in a darkened room. Boys should be out and about, running and jumping and generally making a big nuisance of themselves, she thought.

Then there was the question of her privacy being invaded. Mrs. Davies had nothing to hide from anyone, but no one likes to live as if they are in a goldfish bowl. She found the whole situation far from comfortable.

After two weeks, things took a turn for the worse. Danny decided that the data he was collecting was simply not good enough. Page after page of his notebook was filled with such riveting and vital observations as: "Subject X did not leave house. Subject X not visible. Subject X's movements unknown."

Danny decided that he must get closer to his subject. He didn't mean that he should invite her for tea and try to get to know her. He meant that his position of surveillance should be a lot nearer to her house, so that he had a chance of finding out exactly what she did inside.

Now, Danny's activities were impolite, unneighbourly, almost certainly downright criminal and, in the case of what he did next, extremely stupid.

One evening, as dusk was falling, Danny crept down the road, flattening himself against the walls and railings of the gardens as much as possible (and thereby, I'm afraid, making himself a lot more conspicuous than he would otherwise have been). When he reached Mrs. Davies' house, he very, very carefully pushed open her creaking gate.

Now Mrs. Davies was old and not very steady on her feet, but her eyes and ears were as sharp as ever. She had watched Danny's curious behaviour since he had left his own front garden a few minutes earlier. Now, she watched with horror as the weird boy began to crawl across her front garden on his hands and knees. What on earth did he think he was doing? He looked ridiculous.

Meanwhile, Danny felt that he was making some progress at last. Inch by inch, he reached the front of the house and wiggled himself through a flower bed beneath a downstairs window. Then, very, very slowly, Danny raised his head above the window sill and looked inside.

It was at this point that Mrs. Davies finally felt she had had enough. The boy was a nuisance, even if he hadn't yet done anything really awful. Mrs. Davies made up her mind to confront the snooper herself. She hurried over to the window and flung it open ... *smack!* ... into the face of Danny Dickson, Investigator.

Danny fell back into the flower bed and saw little coloured stars buzzing around his head for a good five minutes. As his vision cleared, he became aware of two things: a horrible pain in his nose and the sight of Mrs. Davies leaning over him and looking very concerned.

"I do hope you're not badly hurt, my boy," she said. "Can you get up?"

Danny wiggled each of his limbs in turn and decided that nothing was broken. As a conclusion, it was wide of the mark. Later that evening, in the casualty department to which Mrs. Davies had insisted on taking him, he was told that he had a broken nose.

"Broken?" gasped Danny. He had not seen himself in a mirror since Mrs. Davies had thwacked him with the frame of the window. He had visions of his nose being squashed flat against his face.

"Don't worry," said the doctor. "Your beauty will be unmarred. I'm going to pack your nose with cotton wool and put a dressing on the tiny cut across the bridge. After two weeks, you'll be fine. Until then, you'll have to breathe through your mouth."

For a couple of days, Danny's nose was a little tender when touched but was otherwise fine. The main difference that Danny and his family noticed was that he lost all interest in food, even the contents of his bag of specially selected surveillance provisions. At first he couldn't understand it. Then he realized that his sense of taste had almost gone. Why on earth would breaking his nose make his taste buds give up? It was Danny's small sister who solved the mystery when she found her brother toying with a plate of chips.

"You'll get your appetite back when the cotton wool comes out of your nose, Danny," she said. "You need a sense of smell to taste things properly. With your nose bunged up, you can't expect to be able to taste. I'm surprised a great private eye like you doesn't know that. I learnt it in school last year."

Danny was relieved but annoyed to be shown up by his own sister. He retired to his room to sulk and think about things.

Sitting in his room reminded the young detective of his ill-starred project to find out about Mrs. Davies. But he was smiling with satisfaction, considering that he had, after all, succeeded, even if it had turned out that Mrs. Davies was doing nothing illegal. The price of a broken nose was a high one, admittedly, but on his return from hospital, Mrs. Davies had invited him into the house. There, he had been fascinated to see the hieroglyphics she worked on, painstakingly deciphering their meanings.

"It's a bit like detective work, I suppose," she had said, with a sly grin at young Danny.

Despite the "success" of his last case, Danny did not want to wait for long before taking on a new project. Luckily, one presented itself almost at once.

The following morning, as the family gathered for breakfast, Danny overheard his parents talking about Hyssop House. This was an imposing building on the other side of the street. It had been lived in by the same family for thirty years, but had recently been let—four times! Each family only seemed to stay for a few weeks—a month at most. Then the house became available again.

"The last lot only lasted ten days," said Danny's mum. "No wonder there's a rumour that the house is haunted."

Danny's dad gave a snort of laughter. "Well, that's one way of putting it." he said.

All of Danny's detective instincts were aroused by this exchange. What was the secret of the house where nobody stayed? Was it really haunted or was there an even more sinister reason? Danny's imagination ran riot. He imagined that the house was the base for a vicious gang of international smugglers. Each time a new family moved in, the smugglers were forced to move out—until they could "persuade" the family to move on again.

Danny couldn't wait for the meal to be over. He had preparations to make!

Later that morning, armed with a new yellow notebook marked "Location X", a tape measure (for trying to find secret rooms and hidden passages) and a couple of cans of juice (instead of his usual bag of provisions), Danny set off for Hyssop House. He had tried to borrow his dad's camera, as well, but his dad was still smarting from the fact that his best binoculars had been returned with half a flower bed obscuring the lenses.

Danny made his way cautiously down the drive. As he entered the gate, the passing postman called out.

"You're a brave man to venture down there!" and pedalled on his way.

Thrilled that he had been seen as an intrepid explorer, Danny crept on. He found that entering the house was no problem at all. The last occupants had left without even closing the front door!

Inside, Hyssop House looked very much as you would imagine an abandoned house to look. It wasn't rotting or falling apart. It simply looked uncared for. There  was also evidence to show that the last family had left in a hurry. A teddy bear, a couple of shoes and even a

half-drunk mug of coffee had been left behind corners. Danny was delighted. Here at last was a real mystery. One that he could get his teeth into. It might be the making of his reputation as a detective.

For the next two hours, Danny roamed the house, writing down every clue he could find. They were clues that seemed completely unrelated, but the boy-detective knew that in the best stories, a keen mind could often see the pattern behind apparently random signs. Why, for example, was so much food left in the larder? Why did there seem to be an enormous number of tubs, cans and bottles of cleaning materials?

Back at home, Danny puzzled over the information he had retrieved. It seemed to make no sense. There was, he was sorry to see, no evidence at all that the house was used by a gang of international smugglers—not unless they were smuggling disinfectant, which seemed pretty unlikely.

For the next two weeks, Danny returned again and again to Hyssop House. He searched every inch of it over and over again. From the mail that was still being delivered, he was able to work out the names of the four families who had most recently lived there (although his mother could have told him this if he had asked). Further than that, Danny felt that his mission had been a failure.

He was still feeling depressed about it when he visited the doctor to have the cotton wool removed from his nose.

That afternoon, after a lunch that he had enjoyed for the first time in a fortnight, Danny returned one last time to Hyssop House. As soon as he went in, he gasped and staggered back. A smell of overwhelming disgustingness filled every room. He could hardly breathe. No wonder no one could live here!

Danny staggered home, gulping great lungfuls of pure air.

"I see you've been to Hyssop House," said his mother. "Why no one has fixed the drains in all this time, I can't imagine. It's a disgrace."

Danny reluctantly felt that he was the disgrace—as a detective. He wondered if it was too late to consider a change of career, and whether Mrs. Davies would consider teaching him all she knew about Egyptian hieroglyphics...

The Musical Mouse

Your first pet is special. Often, that's because of the amount of time it has taken you to persuade strangely reluctant parents to let you have a pet in the first place. Why is it that they can only ever see non-existent problems? When I asked my dad if I could have a lizard, he said, "No way. It will leave hair on the sofa." Oh yes? A *lizard*?

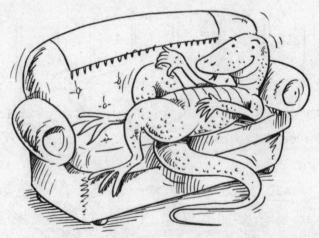

When I mentioned that I would quite like a hamster, Mum said, "That's all very well, Arthur, but I know who'll have to take it for walks when you're too lazy to get out of bed at the weekend. If you think I am going to be dragged around the countryside by a great, slobbering creature like that, you can think again."

Sometimes I think my parents come from prehistoric times. Maybe then giant hamsters stalked the earth. Quite possibly, they slobbered. I'm pretty sure it doesn't happen today. Anyway, I didn't get my hamster *or* my lizard.

I campaigned for a long time for a parrot. I liked the idea that it could talk to me and say rude things about certain people (need I say more?) who never listened to what I was saying. Then, one day at school, we learnt something useful. It's rare that you learn anything useful at that place, so I was pretty surprised. Mrs. Spangler told us that parrots had hugely powerful beaks, which I already knew really. I just hadn't thought what it meant. She said they could crack brazil nuts with one bite. Now, we'd just had a bowl of nuts for Christmas, and I can tell you that it would take a small steamroller to get into one of those things. The thought that a comparatively puny parrot could crack one with ease gave me pause for thought. Could it, for example, snap the tops off my favourite felt pens? Might it crunch into my models of the entire Italian football team? What exactly would happen if it decided to take a bite of a person's earlobe or big toe? The answers, I decided, were *yes*, *YES*, and *OWWWW!* I dropped my parrot campaign there and then. Since my parents hardly seemed to have noticed six long months of steady pressure, they didn't turn a hair (so to speak) when I suddenly began suggesting that a rabbit would really enhance our lives as a family.

"I completely fail to see how," said my father in his usual positive way. "Unless we could eat it when it was nice and plump. My mother often used to cook rabbit."

This was so gross, I could hardly speak. Mum was no better.

"Darling," she said, with her mind on one of her crossword competitions, "it will make a terrible noise, running round on one of those little wheels in the middle of the night. You won't get any sleep."

You see what I mean about parents? I tried hard to get them to understand that the hutch would be outside and there was no question of a little wheel. To be fair, my father did then come up with an almost-sensible objection.

"Arthur," he said, "has it occurred to you that we live on the fourteenth floor of a block of flats. Where exactly do you propose that we put this hutch? Hanging out of the window on a bit of elastic?"

I muttered a bit, but he was right. I pretty much despaired of ever getting a pet of my own right there and then. We're not actually supposed to have animals in the flats at all, because of the noise and mess. Frankly, our neighbours cause more noise and mess than a herd of elephants could possibly make. Mrs. Meliflua sings her ghastly opera at full blast on one side. Hairy Harris (that's not his real name, but it suits him) leaves bits of motorbike on the landing for people to fall over. When we first moved here, Dad did complain about both of them, but nothing happened except that Hairy Harris made several threatening gestures in our direction in the lift and put up a picture of a skull and crossbones on his door. Mrs. Meliflua puts her nose in the air whenever she sees us, which often results in her falling over a bit of motorbike.

Here's another of my observations on life coming up. One day, I'm going to write them all down in a book to save my own children the trouble of learning them by bitter experience themselves. It's this: it's just when you give up hoping for something that it comes along anyway. The very next day after the conversation about the rabbit, my father suggested that I might like him to buy me a mouse.

It was such a surprise that I didn't understand what he was talking about for a while.

"It wouldn't be much good without a computer," I said.

"Don't be a wally, Arthur," he said, "I don't mean that kind of mouse. I mean a little furry thing with pink ears."

"Look," I said, "I haven't played with soft toys for years. Everyone I know would laugh at me. Thanks all the same, but no thanks."

"Arthur, sometimes I think you're on a different planet," said Dad (as if *he* can talk!) "I mean a pet mouse. I mean a little scampering, scuffling thing with a twitchy nose, four feet and a tail. And, in case you think I haven't given this serious consideration, I plan to buy you a cage for it, too. I can't bear the thought of Mrs. Meliflua's screams if it ever escaped into her flat."

Well, I was speechless for a good minute (a record for me, as Dad was quick to point out). I hurried him into the lift before he could change his mind. The pet shop was only round the corner.

I'd been in the pet shop lots of times before, until the owner threw me out for drooling at the lizards and hamsters but never buying anything. He eyed me with a good deal of suspicion now, but Dad was already asking to see some mice, so I didn't have any trouble. At least, not that kind of trouble, but choosing a mouse was pretty difficult. They were all cute. I did try to persuade Dad that mice needed company, but he said I was lucky to get even one, and anyway, I would be its company. In the end, I chose a little white chap with a cheeky face and a way of putting his nose in the air that reminded me of Mrs. Meliflua.

"As long as that's the *only* way he's like her," said Dad, "I don't mind. It's bad enough having one opera-singer on the landing. We don't want two. Now, which cage shall we get?"

I'll say this for Dad, when he makes up his mind to do something, he does it thoroughly. He didn't just buy the smallest, cheapest cage. He said we had to be sure that Squeaky (that's what we decided to call the mouse. I know it's a bit obvious, but it seemed to suit him.) was comfortable. The cage we bought in the end was big enough for several mice. I did mention that, but Dad pretended not to hear.

Squeaky settled into his new home very quickly. He scurried about his cage in a way that made me pretty sure he liked it. He made himself a really cosy little bed in one corner and nibbled at the seeds and things I gave him with enthusiasm. After only a day, I couldn't imagine life without Squeaky. Even Mum and Dad seemed fond of him.

"Now remember," said Mum, when she had watched Squeaky doing his cute little face-washing act, "you absolutely must not take him out of his cage under any circumstances. If he got out into the hallway, who knows what would happen? I'm pretty sure that Hairy Harris would stamp on him and Mrs. Meliflua would probably scream the place down. Though nobody did anything about *his* mess or *her* noise, I bet they'd throw us out for having a pet before Mrs. M.'s screams had

 died down. Luckily, she's away until the end of the month, or I'd have been worried about meeting her when we were bringing all this stuff in."

Over the next few days, I got to know my new friend a bit better. I discovered that he liked apple but not celery. I found that he always washed his ears when he woke up. He liked to run up and down the cage chasing his own tail but sometimes he would stand on two feet in the middle and wave his arms about, almost as though he was conducting an orchestra.

And Squeaky was very good at night. He didn't run around on his wheel or make any kind of noise except a little bit of scuttling and some tiny munching sounds.

It was on Saturday that I found out about Squeaky's other talents. I cleaned out his cage, as I had promised Dad that I would do every single week, and was just watching him doing his standing-in-the-middle-of-the-cage performance when Squeaky started to sing. Yes, sing! I don't mean little squeaking noises that just might be singing, either. It was real music. The kind of thing that Mrs. Meliflua sings when she's in residence.

"*La, la, la, la, la, la, la, LAAAA!*" sang Squeaky, clasping his paws in front of him. I couldn't believe it. Squeaky took up another pose. "*Me, me, me, me, me, me, MEEEEEEEEEEEEE!*" he yodelled. It was amazing. It was extraordinary. It most definitely *wasn't* my sort of music. I edged closer to the cage, thinking that I might be imagining it. The sound grew louder and louder. I opened the window,

to be sure that it wasn't coming from there. Outside, a plane went past, a car hooted in the street, and those impossible kids from number twelve shouted as they skateboarded up and down the pavement. There was no grand opera to be heard.

I don't often consult my parents when I have a problem in life. It's been my experience that their advice is usually twenty years out of date. But in a situation like this, I didn't know which way to turn. I went into the sitting room, where Dad was watching the TV and Mum was about to paint her toenails, and begged them to come and see Squeaky. Something in my tone must have alarmed them, because they both assumed straight away that he was lying in the middle of his cage with his legs in the air.

"No, no!" I said. "He's fine. But he's doing something very odd."

I held my breath as we went into my room. You know how it is if your tooth aches and you go to the dentist? It stops aching the minute you get into the waiting room. I was afraid that when we went back, Squeaky would be doing mouse-like things without an aria to be heard. But for once, the unexpected did happen. Or didn't happen, depending on your point of view. There was Squeaky, standing just as I had left him, and singing his heart out.

"It's unbelievable," I said.

"It's extraordinary," said Dad.

"It's Mozart," said Mum. And she started to sing along with Squeaky. My mum's not very tuneful and she doesn't sound a bit like Mrs. Meliflua, but I could tell that she knew the tune. Squeaky really was singing Mozart. And he was a mouse. And he was in a cage in my bedroom.

We all sat down on my bed. It was partly so we could think and partly because our knees felt a bit wobbly.

"Do you think we're having some kind of hallucination?" asked Dad. "What did you put in that sausage and mash last night, Pru?"

"There was nothing wrong with it," said Mum sharply. She's a bit sensitive about her cooking, probably because she's got a brother who's a chef and acts as though there's no one else in the world who can turn out anything edible.

"It could be that genetic engineering," I suggested. "I saw a programme on TV where they were growing a human ear on a mouse. It was horrible. Maybe they've started growing human vocal chords on them now."

"I think human vocal chords would look as weird as an ear on a mouse," said Mum. "I mean, I think you'd be able to tell. They'd stick out or something."

"I think he *is* getting fatter," I said. "But I thought it was because he liked our food better than the stuff he was getting in the pet shop."

We might have gone on worrying about it for weeks if there hadn't been a knock on the door at that moment. Mum and Dad didn't seem to be able to move,

so I went to answer it. To my surprise, Mrs. Meliflua stood on the doorstep.

"Ah, Arturo," she said (she always talks like that), "are your parents in?"

I led the way to my bedroom and showed her Mum and Dad sitting on the bed looking weird.

"Are they ill?" asked our neighbour.

"No," I said, without thinking. I guess I'm just a naturally truthful person. "They're a bit shocked because my mouse has started singing Mozart."

"Mouse?" said Mrs. Meliflua, her voice rising to singing pitch. I could have kicked myself. In the heat of the moment, I'd completely forgotten about the no-pets rule. But Mrs. Meliflua had moved on from the mouse problem.

"Did you say Mozart?" she asked, going up to the cage. "Good heavens, you're right! It's *Le Nozze di Figaro*."

"Is it, indeed?" said Dad.

"And what's more, I know where it's coming from," said Mrs. Meliflua.

"So do we," said Mum. "It's Squeaky."

"It most certainly is *not* squeaky!" cried our neighbour. "It's the very best equipment that money can buy. That's what I came around to tell you. Firstly that I'm back and secondly that I have bought a new music centre and earphones so that you will no longer have cause to complain when I play my opera."

"But we thought you sang it!" cried Dad. "Do you mean that Squeaky's cage is acting as a kind of receiver?"

"It sounds like it," said Mrs. M., flattered that we had taken her for a great singer. "And no doubt it will do the mouse good, especially in her condition."

Well, yes, it turned out we did need that bigger cage after all. It's just as well we're friends with Mrs. Meliflua now!

The
Missing
Mummy

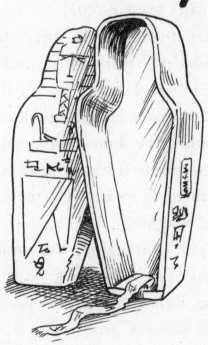

Mrs. Morris looked worried. She sighed several times as she tucked Millie and Max into bed.

"What's the matter, Mum?" asked Millie. "I'll clear up the mess in the bathroom tomorrow, honestly."

"It's not that, pet," said her mother. "It's just that something is bothering me at work. I can't make it out."

Max frowned. He knew that his mum found it hard to make ends meet, and her job as a cleaner at the museum meant a lot to her. She could only clean at nights, when the doors were shut to the public, so Mrs. Evans from next door always came in to sit with the children while she was out.

"Is it something we could help with?" asked Max. "We're good at solving mysteries. Remember how we found your watch for you at Christmas?"

Mrs. Morris had lost her precious watch, one of the last presents the twins' father had given her, on Christmas Day. After interrogating everyone (there was always a houseful at Christmas), Max and Millie decided that the watch must be among all the wrapping paper from the presents. Sure enough, after half an hour of delving and diving and making a huge mess, Millie had spotted the watch at the bottom of the pile.

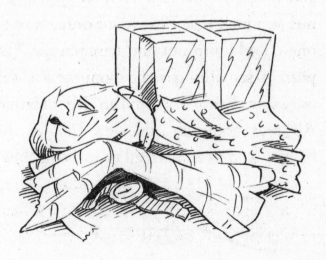

Mrs. Morris smiled.

"You're both great detectives," she said, "but this is a grown-up mystery. You see, no one is supposed to be in the museum at night, except me. But just recently I've found that things have been moved *after* I've cleaned them but before I've gone home. That means there is someone else moving around the museum when I am. I've never seen anyone, but I know that must be so. Alf, the security guard, has never seen anyone either. It's not so much that I'm worried that someone could jump out and frighten me, but what if something went missing? I'm the only one with a key. I'm the only one that Alf sees going in and out. I'll get the blame. And I can't afford to lose this job."

"You should report it to the museum manager," said Millie. "At school, we always have to tell the headteacher if we see something bad or strange. You should do the same. Then they'll know it's not you."

Mrs. Morris looked a lot happier.

"You're absolutely right, Millie," she said. "Clever girl! I'll pop in after I've dropped you both at school tomorrow and see the manager myself. Now, lie down, both of you. Mrs. Evans will be here any minute and I've got work to do."

"You'll be careful, won't you, Mum?" said Millie.

"If there's anything scary, hit it with your mop!" advised Max.

"Goodnight!" laughed their mum.

But Mrs. Morris didn't go to see the museum manager the next day because she didn't come home that night. Mrs. Evans waited until she was quite sure that something was wrong. She tried ringing the museum, but the phones were all switched off for the night. Then she rang the police. They promised to go round to the museum straight away to see what had happened.

Alf, the security guard, was sitting at his post just inside the front door.

"We're looking for Mrs. Mary Morris," the first policeman explained. "We understand that she works here."

"Oh yes, I know Mary," replied Alf Gardner, "but you'll find her at home now. She left over an hour ago. Look, this is where she signed herself out in the book. Here."

"The signature looks pretty shaky to me," said the second policeman. "Was she okay when she left here?"

"Oh, she was in a hurry," said Alf. "She always likes to get back to her kids as soon as she can. But she does a good job, mind you. The old place has never looked as clean and well-kept as it does these days. I can give you her address, if you like. I've got it here somewhere."

But the policemen exchanged a glance and said goodnight. They already knew where Mrs. Morris lived, and they knew that she wasn't home. Carefully, they retraced her path through the dark streets, but there was no sign of the missing woman at all.

As soon as he saw Mrs. Evans getting breakfast in the kitchen next morning, Max knew that something was wrong.

"Where's Mum?" cried Millie.

Mrs. Evans decided that it was best to tell the truth.

"You mustn't worry, my dears," she said, "there's probably a very good reason why your mother hasn't come home. Maybe she stopped to help someone who was hurt. You know what she's like. And she hasn't been able to get to a phone to let us know."

"Mum would always let us know," said Max, suddenly sounding much older than he looked. "Something's happened to her and we need to speak to the police."

"I've already done that, dear," said Mrs. Evans. "They're looking into it right now. They'll soon find her, I'm sure."

"No, I mean that Millie and I have important information," said Max. "I'm going to call them myself, right now. Mum showed us how to do it, didn't she, Millie? Come on!"

It wasn't long before Max and Millie were telling the story of their mother's worries to the police.

"That's very interesting," they were told. "We'll make enquiries straight away."

But a couple of hours later, the police called at the house.

"I'm sorry, kids," said Sergeant Fox. "The security guard says he doesn't know anything about any prowler at night. He reckons your mum never mentioned it to him. Do you think maybe she kept it to herself until she was sure?"

"Maybe," said Millie doubtfully. "But I'm pretty sure she meant that she'd discussed it with this Alf. He can't be telling the truth!"

"He's worked there for twenty years," said the policeman, "and there's never been so much as a teaspoon missing. I think he's pretty reliable. He's coming up to retirement age. I don't think he'll do anything to put his pension in danger. Do you have any other ideas?"

Max and Millie looked at each other. They did have ideas, but they didn't want to share them just yet.

"Mrs. Evans is going to stay with you until we find your mum," said the policeman. "Try not to worry. It's not as easy as all that to lose a whole grown-up person. We'll find her."

As soon as the police had gone, Max and Millie went to sit in their treehouse and discuss their next step.

"I don't know about you, but I don't like the sound of this Alf character," said Max. "I'm sure Mum talked to him. If there *was* an intruder in the museum, then Alf isn't doing his job properly. Or maybe he's letting someone in. And if there isn't anyone coming into the museum, then the person moving things around has to be Alf himself. Either way, he's involved in this somehow."

"I agree," said Millie, "and the other thing I think is that we've got to go over there and have a look around. We can't find out anything staying here. And you know, Mum said we were good detectives herself. Let's slip out tonight."

Late that night, Mrs. Evans put the twins to bed and told them for the twentieth time not to worry. It was a silly thing to say, really. Of course, they were worried. But they knew they would feel a whole lot better as soon as they started *doing* something about it.

It wasn't difficult to creep out without disturbing Mrs. Evans. The poor woman had hardly slept the night before and was now stretched out on the sofa in the living room, snoring gently.

Max and Millie hurried through the deserted streets towards the museum. If they saw anyone coming, they scurried into a shop doorway. At last, the great big doors of the museum loomed above them at the top of a flight of steps.

Millie and Max peered cautiously through the windows in the doors. They could see Alf, the security guard, sitting at his desk reading the paper and drinking a cup of coffee.

"He's not paying much attention to the monitors on his desk," hissed Millie. "Anything could be going on and he'd never notice."

"Let's hope that's true," said Max. "Now, remember that loose basement window Mum told us about? Come on!"

It wasn't long before Max and Millie were inside the museum. Although many of the lights were on, it still seemed very dark and different at night. The twins had been there lots of times during the day, looking at interesting exhibits that their mother had talked about, but there had always been people about and excited chatter in front of the main display cases.

"What should we do?" asked Millie.

Max looked uncertain, too.

"I'm not sure," he said. "I think we should just walk around and look out for anything that's out of place. We know these galleries well enough. We should notice. But we'll have to be careful to look out for the cameras that send pictures to Alf's monitors."

"That's easy," said Millie. "They're in the same place in each room, and what's more, they are set for people a lot taller than us. If we work our way along the wall in each gallery, they won't be able to spot us."

"Then let's get going!" whispered Max. "I think we should stick together, don't you?"

"That's probably a good idea," agreed Millie, hoping she sounded as though she didn't mind too much either way. She really didn't want to be on her own in this spooky building.

Everything seemed to be in its place in the costume gallery. Although they looked rather ghostly at night, the models in their costumes and the suits of armour at the end all looked untouched.

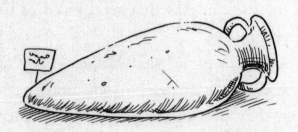

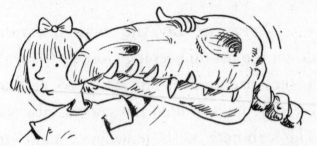

It was the same story in the gallery where the Greek and Roman finds were kept. The vases, bowls and piles of coins stood silent and still.

In the gallery with prehistoric remains, massive dinosaur fossils looked as they always did. For the first time in their lives, Max and Millie didn't stop to gaze and gasp at them. They had more important things to think about.

As soon as they entered the gallery with ancient Egyptian displays, Millie stiffened and stopped.

"There's definitely something different here," she hissed. "Don't you feel it?"

Max nodded.

Very carefully, the children moved down the room, keeping close to the wall as they had agreed. The stones covered in hieroglyphics looked the same as always. The cabinets with jewellery, make-up boxes and little statues seemed fine, too. But in the centre of the room, something was dreadfully wrong.

In the middle of the floor there always stood a huge wooden casket, taken from an Egyptian tomb. It was beautifully decorated, with gold and precious stones, and showed the calm face of a pharaoh, his arms crossed in front of him. Many times when they visited the museum, Max and Millie had discussed whether there was a mummy inside the casket. Now they wondered even more, for the casket was open, its great lid swung back on its hinges to show the dark and empty inside—and a single piece of bandage.

"D-d-d-do you think there was something inside it?" asked Max.

"Y-y-y-you mean, something that's out here with us now?" stammered Millie. "I don't know. I really wish I did."

"In any case, this proves that there's something going on," said Max, feeling a little better now he knew that Millie was as frightened as he was. "I'm sure this isn't meant to be open. But why hasn't Alf noticed? I'm more suspicious of him than ever. Isn't he supposed to do rounds or something, so that he can make sure everything is all right all the way through the museum? Shhhh! I think I can hear him coming now! Let's hide behind this cabinet. Quick!"

The children were only just in time. Thudding footsteps echoed through the gallery, coming closer and closer. Millie peeped out from their hiding place and clamped her hand over her mouth so that she wouldn't scream.

"Is it Alf?" whispered Max.

"No. Yes. Maybe!" Millie had never sounded so frightened. Max peeped out himself and gasped. Lumbering towards them down the gallery was a huge mummy. Ancient bandages covered him from head to foot. There were dark holes where his eyes should have been. His great arms swung stiffly by his sides. And he seemed to be heading straight for the twins' hiding place!

Millie felt rather than saw the huge shadow fall over them. Very, very slowly she raised her eyes and looked straight into the mummy's fearsome face.

But Max, still looking at the mummy's feet, saw something even more breathtaking. Peeping out from under the bandages, he was pretty sure he saw a glimpse of dark blue uniform. Quick as a flash, he lunged forward and grabbed a loose piece of bandage around the mummy's ankle, pulling and pulling as hard as he could.

Max had only meant to see if the bandages came away, but his move was even more successful. Wrapped up in his stiff bandages, the mummy found it hard to keep his balance. As Max pulled, his feet slipped out from under him and he fell, banging his bandaged head on a carved stone.

"Ow!" The mummy said a few very unpleasant words that were definitely not ancient Egyptian. Millie raced forward and tied the loose bandage to the leg of a cabinet. Max did the same with the other leg and the two arms. There was no way that the mummy could move now.

Max's face was grim as he seized the bandages around the mummy's head and pulled them away. A familiar face appeared.

"Alf Gardner!" cried Max. "I knew it! What have you done with our mum?"

Alf spluttered and spat.

"Interfering brats! Why couldn't you leave things alone? Your mother was just the same. Always asking questions and interfering. I'll be retiring in a few weeks time and do you know how big my pension will be? Not enough for a flea to live on! I was just going to help myself to one or two bits and pieces to make me comfortable in my old age. I should have known you two would take after your mother."

"Where is she?" Max was talking through clenched teeth. "What have you done with her?"

"Oh, she's okay," said the guard. "Another day and I would have been gone. Then you'd have found her, safe and well. She's shut up in the storeroom at the end of the prehistoric gallery. Trussed up with all the old bones in there."

But Max and Millie were off before he'd even finished speaking.

"Mum! Mum!" yelled Millie, heaving open the storeroom door.

"Mmmmmfnnng!"

Inside, Mrs. Morris was bound and gagged. Her eyes filled with tears as she glimpsed her children.

"Oh my dears," she cried, as Millie tore the gag from her mouth, "I thought I'd never see you again. How worried you must have been. I'm so sorry!"

But the twins were crying, too, so relieved that they couldn't speak.

"Hey, untie me!" laughed their mother. "How can I hug you trussed up like this?"

The police shook their heads when they heard how Millie and Max had taken matters into their own hands, but they were impressed, too. So was the museum manager.

"It seems to me that you've a lot to offer us," he told Mrs. Morris. "Brains and bravery run in the family. How would you feel about becoming our Head of Security? There would be a big rise in salary, of course. When could you start?"

"As soon as you like," smiled Mrs. Morris. "With two great detectives like this to live up to, I'd better get some practice right away!"

The
Hidden
Homework

Mrs. Closter looked even more severe than usual—and that's really saying something. She has a face like an unripe lemon at the best of times.

"You know what I'm going to ask you, Angela," she said. "But I can only guess at your reply. *Where is it?*"

Angela gave a charming smile.

"My homework, Mrs. Closter?"

"Absolutely," the teacher confirmed.

"Well," said Angela, smiling again, "it's the most extraordinary thing."

"I don't doubt it." Mrs. Closter's tone could have sliced ham.

"You see," Angela was getting into her stride now, "my little cousin Hugo came to stay yesterday and he's only just learning to use his potty. Unfortunately…"

"Stop right there!" cried Mrs. Closter holding up a magisterial hand. "I think we can all guess where this is leading, and I think I speak for the whole class when I say *we don't want to hear it*. The gist of the matter, as usual, is that you have failed to give in your homework. Last week, the dog ate it. The week before, a mysterious fire in your home burnt only the homework and nothing else at all. Before that, we had a freak hurricane in your garden, a strange mould growing in your bedroom, and a hamster who needed a nest."

"It's very odd, isn't it?" Angela gave an unconvincing giggle. "These things don't happen to my homework for any other classes. It's only maths homework. I can't imagine why."

"My guess," said Mrs. Closter coldly, "would be pretty simple. My guess would be that if a certain person hasn't actually *done* her homework, it's much more likely that some extraordinary disaster will befall it. What do you have to say about that?"

"I really don't know, Mrs. Closter," said Angela sweetly. "You see, I *always* do my homework."

Now this, as you have probably guessed, was not strictly true. Angela always did her geography homework, her history homework and her English homework. She almost *never* did her maths homework. The reason, as you have probably also guessed, was that Angela was not very good at maths. She didn't understand what she was supposed to do most of the time. Here Mrs. Closter must be held at least partly to blame. She was an excellent teacher for the brightest and best pupils in the class, but she had very little time for those who were less confident. She tended to think they weren't trying or were lazy instead of realizing that they simply had lost track of what she was saying about fifteen minutes earlier.

Over the weeks that followed the explanations for missing homework that Angela came up with became more and more extraordinary.

"My granny used it to light the fire," she said one week.

"My mother had new covers put on the sofa and unfortunately my homework was lying on a cushion," she tried.

"My dad borrowed it to read on the train and left it in the luggage rack," was another suggestion.

Pretty soon, Mrs. Closter made a point of enquiring into the health of Angela's homework as soon as she stepped into the class.

"How's the homework, Angela?" she would ask. "Eaten by an alligator? Made into jam by your granny? Caught up in a tidal wave and washed all the way to Japan?"

Angela would shake her head, but in truth her own explanations were only slightly less fantastical.

It was just at this point that a new girl joined the class. Her name was Clara and she turned out to be extraordinarily good at maths. Of course, she became Mrs. Closter's favourite at once.

"Does anyone know the answer to problem three?" the teacher would ask. "Robert? Damian? Angela? No, I thought not. Now, Clara, perhaps you can tell us."

And Clara always could.

You might think that Clara's maths abilities would make her unpopular with the rest of the class, but the opposite was true. This was partly because Clara was a jolly, fun-loving girl who tried to make friends with everyone. However, it was mainly because Clara regularly helped everyone with their homework on the bus on the way to school.

Strangely enough, although Clara was nice to everyone, she soon became special friends with Angela. It wasn't long

before Clara asked Angela about the famous missing homework mystery.

"Those things don't really happen, do they?" she asked.

"Well, only in a sort of a way," said Angela evasively.

"Shall I take that as a 'no'?" smiled Clara. "So why don't you just do the homework? It wouldn't take that long."

"Oh but I do!" cried Angela. She had been telling stories about it for so long that she could hardly bring herself to stop.

"No, you don't," said Clara firmly. "What I want to know is, why not?"

Angela hung her head. It was hard to confess, even to a friend. At last she managed to whisper the problem.

"I don't understand the questions, usually," she said. "Then I'm scared of getting the answers wrong. I'm pretty sure Mrs. Closter would laugh at me."

"Well, you could be right about that," said Clara grimly, "but, you know, there's nothing very hard about maths. Why don't you let me show you one or two things? It's easy—really!"

After an hour or two of explaining some simple problems to Angela, Clara began to have a little more sympathy for Mrs. Closter. Angela had got the idea so firmly into her head that she didn't understand maths, she very often didn't even try. However, Clara was not a girl to give up easily. Day after day, she took Angela off to a quiet corner at lunchtime and showed her the mysteries of maths. Very, very slowly, Angela began to see what she was talking about. At last the day came when Clara started to explain something and Angela said, without thinking too hard about it, "No, no, I already know that. The answer is $a + b$."

Clara laughed, fell back in mock exhaustion and said, "At last! My work is done! How about having a go at that homework tonight, Algebra Angela? It didn't look too difficult to me."

"Well, it wouldn't, would it?" said Angela. "But I'll give it a try. Let's meet before class in the morning and you can check what I've done."

"Sorry," said Clara. "I'll have to see you in class. I've got another five maths-muddlers to help before school."

That night, Angela tackled her homework and found it nothing like as frightening as she had feared. She looked with pride at the neat rows of figures in her exercise book.

"If Mrs. Closter's got a weak heart, I may be about to change our maths classes for ever," said Angela gruesomely.

Next morning, when Mrs. Closter called for homework to be handed in, Angela went up with all the rest and added her exercise book to the pile. Mrs. Closter, weak heart or no weak heart, noticed right away and at once dived on the pile of books and extracted Angela's.

"Ah ha!" cried the teacher. "I am holding in my hand an extremely rare item, notably a piece of homework from Angela Sparkes Rogers. It deserves to go into the school museum, to be enjoyed by posterity, but instead I am simply going to mark it. Now, let's look, which page is it on, Angela?"

"The last one," said Angela, trying hard to sound polite. Mrs. Closter made her madder than any other person she knew. It was at times like this that she remembered why.

Mrs. Closter turned to the last page and grew very red in the face.

"Is this your idea of a joke?" she spluttered, shaking the book in the air. "What happened, Angela? Surely you didn't run out of excuses, did you?"

"What do you mean?" Angela looked surprised and bewildered. But since she had been pretending surprise and bewilderment in Mrs. Closter's class for the last six months, it didn't impress the teacher one bit.

"Perhaps you'd like to find it for me," said Mrs. Closter, handing Angela the book. "The homework, I mean."

Angela turned confidently to the last used page and then stared. That wasn't her homework! Desperately, she began

$$57 + 135 - 72 \div 3 = 40$$

$$\begin{array}{r} 7 \\ 14\ + \\ \hline 21 \end{array} \qquad z + y = 2x \qquad \begin{array}{r} 77 \\ 18\ - \\ \hline 59 \end{array}$$

leafing through, but the homework wasn't there at all.

"I'm sorry," she gasped. "I think I must have put it in another exercise book. I have done it, honestly. I'll look when I get home. I'm sure I'll find it. I'll give it to you in the morning."

"Well done, Angela," replied the teacher in a voice heavy with sarcasm. "You've managed to find another way out of the homework trap. I wondered what you would do when you couldn't think of any more excuses. This is good, very good. I expect your English teacher is really pleased with you. I would guess that your imaginative writing is first class.

If only the same could be said about your maths! Go and sit down."

Angela went back to her seat with a frown on her face. At lunchtime, after an accusing look from Clara, she promised her friend that it was true. She *had* done her homework, but she must have brought the wrong exercise book to school. That evening, when she got home, Angela searched in vain through every exercise book she could find, even the ones labelled "Poetry" or "Spanish verbs".

There was no sign of the maths homework. Angela began to worry that she had imagined doing it in the first place. She decided to take precautions next time.

When Mrs. Closter handed out homework the next time, Angela took Clara home with her and made her watch while she did the homework in front of

her. Clara thought this was taking things a bit far, but she duly noted that Angela had finished all six questions and which notebook she had written them in.

"Now I want you to take the book," said Angela, "so that I don't lose it accidentally between tonight and maths class tomorrow."

"That's ridiculous!" laughed Clara. "How could you possibly lose it? But if you insist, I will take it. See you in the morning, maths maniac!"

But Angela didn't see Clara in the morning. It seemed that she had been taken ill with a bad cold during the night and wouldn't be back in school for the rest of the week.

"So, Angela," said Mrs. Closter, "have you done your homework?"

"Yes, Mrs. Closter," said Angela with absolute truthfulness.

"Then where is it?" screeched Mrs. Closter. "I'm fast losing my patience with you, young lady. Oh, Clara has it, does she? How very, very convenient for you. You will stay behind after class and do some extra questions during breaktime. This ridiculous state of affairs simply cannot go on."

It *was* a ridiculous state of affairs, and it got worse. Next time, Angela gave her homework to her mum to keep overnight. Her mum, at the end of a long and tiring day, put it in the washing machine with Angela's brother's dirty jeans. Very little of the blue-and-silver-covered exercise book survived.

A week later, Angela did her homework before she even left school and put the exercise book in her locker to be picked up in the morning. Naturally, the caretaker had to choose that very night to check the lockers for all the doorknobs and coathooks missing from the school. In the process, Angela's exercise book tumbled out of the locker and into the caretaker's bucket of soapy water. Another fine mess.

"You know what I think?" asked Clara. "I think it's fate getting its own back on you. As soon as the scales are equal, your homework will stop going missing. Don't worry."

But Angela did worry. After all, she remembered all the many times when she had "mislaid" her homework before. She, more than anyone (except, of course, Mrs. Closter) knew that she had a long way to go before the score was even.

But, strange as it may seem, the very thing that was driving Angela mad, also proved to be her saviour. For one sunny afternoon, after interrogating Angela about the homework that the juggernaut outside the school had run over (yes, really!), Mrs. Closter finally lost her icy composure—and when she lost it, she really lost it!

The headmaster came to see what all the shrieking about and persuaded Mrs. Closter to go home and rest. No one was very disappointed when, later in the term, the class was told that Mrs. Closter had decided to retire and would not be returning.

It can't have been a coincidence, can it, that the same afternoon, five of Angela's exercise books suddenly began to overflow with the answers to problems? Her homework was hidden no more.

Vanishing
Vera

Mike didn't usually read the paper. He thought it was a grown-up thing full of boring business news and other stuff he wasn't at all interested in. But for the past week he had been the first to pick up the paper in the morning and often disappeared into the bathroom with it so he wouldn't have to fight his father for the opportunity to read it first. He was fascinated, as many of his friends at school

were, by the story that had dominated the news for the past week and a half. It concerned the mysterious disappearance of Elliot Z. Jakes, master magician and illusionist.

The facts were perfectly simple. While staying with a friend in a chalet in the mountains, Elliot Z. Jakes had taken to going on long walks by himself. His friend reported that he seemed unhappy and talked often of the pressures that being so famous created. He was tired, he said, of not being able to walk down the street without being pestered by fans who wanted his autograph, his trademark multi-coloured scarf, or the secrets on which he had based his career. The friend pointed out that it was these fans who had given Elliot Z. Jakes the wealthy and lifestyle that he so much enjoyed. But the illusionist still seemed upset. The friend hoped that his time in the mountains would give Elliot a chance to rest.

The night before Elliot Z. Jakes disappeared there was a heavy snowstorm. The two friends sat in their chalet talking about old times, when they had been at school together. Elliot went to bed early, saying that he wanted to be up early to prepare to return to his home. He felt, he said, much better and knew now what he had to do to get his life back on track.

Next morning, Elliot's friend awoke to find that the illusionist had already left the chalet. His bags were neatly packed and labelled in the hall, but of the famous magician there was no sign. The friend assumed that he had gone for one last walk before asking for a lift to the station with his bags.

He was wrong.

When Elliot had not returned to the chalet by lunchtime, his friend became worried. When the afternoon passed and

darkness began to fall, he became so alarmed that he called the police. But it was too late that night to start searching the mountains. Instead, checks were made to see if anyone had left the area by train, plane or car that day. Several people had, of course, but none of them sounded at all like Elliot Z. Jakes.

The next day, at first light, the search resumed. It wasn't long before, in the untouched snow in front of the chalet, a set of footprints was picked up. Their size matched the boots and shoes in Elliot's packing. The trackers followed the footprints up the mountainside for several miles. Then, as suddenly as they had appeared, the prints disappeared. In the middle of a snowy wasteland, where no other footprints or marks of any kind were to be seen, the footprints suddenly stopped. There was no sign that the snow had been disturbed, but still the only thing that the rescue team could think of doing was to dig. But they found nothing. Apart from the footprints, there was nothing to show that Elliot Z. Jakes had ever been there.

Although these discoveries were reported on the day after the magician's disappearance, and the story ran for weeks, this was really a triumph of the journalists' ability to make a very few

facts stretch to a lot of words. There were
interviews with Elliot Z. Jakes' magical
assistant, his hairdresser, the man who
made his magic wands and his old mother,
who lived in Tennessee. There was nothing
more to say about *how* the illusionist had
gone missing. The police investigated
every sighting of the missing man from
Brazil to Brighton, but all of them turned
out to be perfectly ordinary people going
about their ordinary business. Elliot Z.
Jakes had apparently disappeared from the
face of the earth, leaving not a trace.

This was the story that Mike was following so avidly in the bathroom each morning, while his father and his sister Ellen hammered on the door with various needs of their own.

Mike had his own ideas about how the magician's last great illusion had been achieved. He was less sure about why. If Elliot Z. Jakes had wanted to retire, why hadn't he just returned to one of his palatial mansions around the world and stayed there? It doesn't take long for the public to forget someone who has been terribly famous if he or she just stays at home and doesn't do anything. After all, no star would need to pay for lots of publicity if being a star was enough by itself to ensure that fans queued on your doorstep every morning. Perhaps, thought Mike, it was simply professional pride that had caused the master magician to make his final act a particularly spectacular one. "Always leave the audience wanting more," Mike's drama teacher used to say. In this case, the public certainly did want more.

While Mike was still avidly reading every line he could lay his hands on about the mysterious disappearance, Aunt Vera came to stay. She was a very, very old lady—not Jake's aunt, or even Jake's dad's aunt, but Jake's grandad's aunt. But she was as spry as she was sharp.

"Now, what's this you're reading, Mike?" she said the morning after she arrived. "An old woman like me doesn't have a bladder of steel, you know."

Mike blushed. He really didn't think that old people should go around talking about bladders. Well, he didn't think that anyone should go around talking about bladders. It just wasn't something you wanted to hear about before your breakfast—or after it, come to that.

Mike told Aunt Vera about the missing magician.

"Poo!" said his aunt rudely. "I can think of dozens and dozens of ways it could have happened. I don't know why everyone is making such a fuss about it."

"Such as what?" asked Mike. "I was thinking of a helicopter myself."

"Not a bad idea, young Mike," said Aunt Vera. "But wouldn't the rotor blades blow the snow about? You'd probably see blurring of the footprints nearest to the site of the disappearance."

Mike was impressed that his aunt knew about rotor blades. As if she could hear what he was thinking, Aunt Vera said sharply, "I'm just old, Mike, not stuck in the Dark Ages. I have heard of helicopters, you know."

"I've thought about the rotor blade problem myself, actually," said Mike. "I would guess that if Elliot Z. Jakes was winched up to the helicopter on a really long line, so that the helicopter could stay high, then the snow wouldn't be disturbed. At least, not more than could be accounted for by a light wind. I looked up the weather for the region, too, and there *was* a light wind that day."

"Good work," said Aunt Vera, "but I think my ideas are more exciting. How about a hot-air balloon? It wouldn't disturb the snow at all, as long as it didn't land."

"I thought about that, too," said Mike, "but it's hard to believe that anyone would *plan* to escape in a hot-air balloon. They're just not very easy to manoeuvre. And the weather can be a problem, too. A friend of mine had a flight booked with his granny and it was cancelled three times because the weather was wrong. And it's so terribly noticeable and not as quiet as

people think. There's one that comes over here sometimes and the gas-burners make a terribly loud noise."

"All right, not a balloon then. Your reasoning is good, young Mike," said his aunt, "although I still think a balloon is a lot quieter than a helicopter. Now I shall have to tell you my own favourite theory. An eagle!"

"An eagle?"

"Yes, a big one, obviously. It could swoop down, clutch Elliot Z. Jakes in its

powerful claws and carry him off without leaving a trace."

Mike had so many objections to this that he hardly knew where to start.

"Are there eagles that big?" he said, as a beginning.

"There are eagles that can scoop up monkeys," said his aunt, "and, I don't know if you know this, but Elliot Z. Jakes was a remarkably small man."

"Still, you couldn't *train* an eagle to come and pick you up," said Mike.

"Who said anything about training? Maybe it was just one of those things that happened out of the blue. There's not a scrap of evidence to suggest that Elliot *planned* to disappear."

"I suppose not," said Mike slowly. "But, well, wouldn't they have found … er … bits of him by now?"

"Not if the eagle has a nest high up in the mountains," smiled his aunt. "Don't look so worried, Mike, I don't seriously think that magician was seized by a giant bird. And yes, I do think he planned to disappear. I never liked that man. I always thought he looked too full of himself when I saw him on TV. I think he's quite definitely responsible for all this and I also think he's enjoying every minute of it."

"So how did he do it, then?" asked Mike. "Have you got any more good ideas?"

"Better than that," said his aunt. "I'll *show* you how it was done. And what's more, I know exactly where the little weasel who caused all this fuss is right now."

Mike looked impressed, but he didn't really believe her. She looked mysterious when he pressed her further and told him that he would see tomorrow.

The next morning, two things made Mike forget all about the missing magician for a while. The first was the fact that it snowed during the night and kept snowing the next morning. It was the first snow of the season in that part of the world, and Mike was very excited. Even better was the fact that Mike's friend Ellen came back from visiting a distant cousin. She arrived, laughing and covered with snow, halfway through the morning.

"It's supposed to stop by lunchtime," she said. "Then we can go outside and play. It's the kind of snow that sticks together, so we can make a snowman."

Aunt Vera was dozing in a corner. She opened one eye when she heard this and smiled to herself.

The family had lunch together and, sure enough, just as they were finishing, the snow stopped and the sun came out. Mike and Ellen leapt up from the table at once, but Aunt Vera held up a hand.

"I know you want to be getting out there," she said, "but I wonder if you could just wait a minute. I'd like to walk down to the end of the garden and I'm not so steady on my feet these days, especially in the snow. I just need to go and ... er ... powder my nose, but I'll be back in a minute. I only need to walk down to the gate and back, just to get a bit of air."

The children felt slightly impatient, but of course they said, "No problem." Aunt Vera shuffled off to ... er ... powder her nose.

Ten minutes later, when she hadn't returned, Mike's mum looked a little concerned and said, "I do hope she hasn't got stuck or anything. I'll just pop up and see what she's doing."

She came down again a few seconds later looking flustered. "She's not in the bathroom and I've checked all the bedrooms," she panted, "but she's nowhere to be seen. "She didn't come back into here, did she?"

Everyone shook their heads. Another search of the house was carried out. Ellen even looked in the cupboard under the stairs and got bumped on the nose by a mop, but of Aunt Vera there was no sign.

"Maybe she forgot she asked us to wait and went out by herself," suggested Mike. He was dying to get outside. "Come on, Ellen! Let's go and look."

There was no sign of Aunt Vera in
the front garden. The even, untouched
snow stretched down to the road. Ellen
and Mike ran round to the back and at
once stopped in their tracks.

Leading from the back door was a
set of footprints, looking distinctly as if
they could belong to Aunt Vera. They
meandered, step by step, into the middle
of the lawn. And stopped.

Mike looked down in astonishment.

"I don't believe it," he said. "She
told me she would show me, and she has!"

He looked all around, to see if there
was a place that the old lady could have
jumped to. But the flowerbeds showed no
signs of disturbance and were five metres
away in all directions. Surely a ninety-
year-old woman couldn't make jumps like
that? Besides, it was clear that the footprints were made by simple walking, not

with the kind of force needed to launch yourself halfway across a garden. Mike looked long and hard at the footprints but he couldn't for the life of him think how she had done it.

"So where is she?" asked Ellen. "She can't have just disappeared into thin air."

"I don't suppose she can," said Mike, "but in any case, I don't think we'll have to wait long to find out. If I know Aunt Vera, she'll want to show how clever she's been. And, to be fair, I want to know, too. Let's go back into the house for a minute and wait."

Although Ellen protested about the snowman she had planned, Mike insisted. Although he didn't think that Aunt Vera would make her surprise last all afternoon, he wasn't quite prepared for hearing her cheery greeting as he went back into the kitchen.

"Hello, my dears!" she called from her comfortable chair in the sitting room. "I'm sorry I forgot you were waiting for me. As you saw, I didn't get as far as the gate after all."

"All right," replied Mike, "I give up, how did you do it? And where is Elliot Z. Jakes?"

"Do you really not know? It's the oldest trick in the book, Mike. I simply walked backwards in my own footprints!"

Mike laughed, then frowned.

"Yes, but that means you're back here. Elliot isn't back in the chalet. They would have looked."

"Isn't he? What about this friend he's supposed to be staying with? I don't suppose anyone even noticed him when Elliot was around. And anyone who can manage magic can manage a little make-up and a false beard. My advice to the police would be to question the so-called friend. From what I could see of Elliot Z. Jakes, he wasn't a man that anyone would want to be friends with."

Aunt Vera was right, of course. Elliot announced his trick to the press the following week. He got lots of publicity, naturally, but I hear that he still doesn't have a friend in the world...

The
Bungling
Burglar

Strangely enough, it wasn't Graham or his dad or his mum who first noticed that the house had been burgled. It was Alphonse. Most of the time, the Norman family thought of Alphonse as a huge but useless hound who ate them out of house and home and had no idea how to behave with decent furniture. Luckily, the Normans didn't have any decent furniture.

This time, however, Alphonse had something of a triumph. As soon as the family came down to breakfast, he began acting in a strange way—well, stranger than usual anyway. He made sure that his audience was fully assembled, trotted over to the corner of the room, sat down, lifted up his head and howled. It was a howl that might have summoned long-lost wolf ancestors from the dead. It was a howl that made Mrs. Norman cover her ears and Mr. Norman drop his coffee. It was a sound unlike anything that Alphonse had made in the past three years, since he had arrived as a puppy.

Graham hurried over to the dog and crouched down.

"What's the matter, Alf?" he asked. "Have you got a pain somewhere. Is it your teeth? Is it your tummy? A splinter in your paw? Someone trod on your tail?" (At this point, Graham looked accusingly at his father, who had been known to be careless about how he placed his feet near Alphonse's basket.)

Alphonse responded by hanging his head and looking up in a beseeching way.

"Give me a clue, Alf," pleaded his master. "Where does it hurt?"

Alphonse cast his eyes upwards, as if to say, "For goodness sake, I'm not in *pain*. I'm trying to tell you something perfectly simple and why you're too dense to spot it for yourselves, I can't imagine." Then he clambered wearily to his feet and trotted across the room to stand with his nose pointed towards the fireplace.

The eyes of the family followed the dog, and it was then that Mrs. Norman spotted what was wrong.

"My lady!" she cried. "My dancing lady! Oh no!"

Lying in the hearth was a figurine of a lady in a blue crinoline twirling around. It was an ornament that Mrs. Norman loved very much, even if her enthusiasm was not shared by the rest of the family. Now, the lady lay there—minus her arms.

"Oh dear," said Mr. Norman and tried to keep a blank look on his face.

This was too much for his wife.

"Oh, that's typical," she said. "If it was something of yours that was broken, we'd all have to go into mourning for a month. If anyone touched one of your precious CDs, there'd be a full-scale post-mortem and an investigation that Scotland Yard would be proud of. But just because it's my ornament and something you didn't care for, it's 'Oh dear'! Thank you very much!"

Mr. Norman tried to retrieve the situation by going to fetch the brush and dustpan, but his wife seized them fiercely.

"Leave her alone!" she cried in a way that betrayed the years she had spent at drama school twenty years earlier.

It was only when the family was back at the breakfast table that Graham wondered out loud how the accident could possibly have happened.

"The lady was quite heavy," he said, "and high up on the mantelpiece. I don't see how she could have fallen down. A breeze or a slammed door wouldn't have done it. And it's much too high for Alf to have jumped up."

"That's right," said Mrs. Norman. "How *could* it have happened? Let's go and look."

Gazing wistfully at their cooling breakfasts, Graham and his dad got up and followed her into the next room. In silence and very dutifully, they examined the scene of the crime. They all agreed that there was no way the figurine could have fallen by accident, unless, as Mr. Norman suggested, there had been a freak earth tremor the night before.

"But none of my other ornaments have fallen down," said Mrs. Norman. "Surely a tremor wouldn't just knock over one figurine? In any case, wouldn't Alphonse have howled *then*?"

Mr. Norman embarked on a lengthy explanation of resonance and sympathetic vibrations but he was out of his depth and the other two members of his family could see that clearly.

"It's a mystery and that's all," said Mr. Norman at last. The family returned to the kitchen to find that Alphonse had eaten all the breakfasts and removed himself from the scene.

"Not much mystery here," said Mrs. Norman grimly, surveying an eggy pawprint on the tablecloth.

Next morning, Alphonse was shut in the hallway when Mrs. Norman, the last member of the family to go to bed, carefully shut all the doors and went upstairs herself. The next morning, as the first person downstairs, she gave a wail of distress that brought a sleepy Mr. Norman and a curious Graham running.

"What is it, Mum?" asked Graham. "Is Alf all right?"

"More than all right," replied Mrs. Norman drily, "I should say."

She nodded her head towards the sitting room. Alphonse was lying asleep on the sofa, which was strictly forbidden.

"What I want to know," said Mrs. Norman, looking accusingly at her son and her husband, "is how he got in there. I'm absolutely certain that I shut the sitting room door last night before I went to bed."

"Clever old Alphonse must have learned to lift the latches with his nose," said Mr. Norman.

Mrs. Norman was not impressed.

"Sometimes I wonder if you and I have been living in the same house for the last twenty years, Richard," she said. "Has it entirely escaped your attention that all our doors have knobs, not latches? I utterly fail to see how a dog could have learnt to turn the knobs. In any case, they're quite stiff. And as if that wasn't enough, the doors were *closed* when I came downstairs this morning."

"Well, Mum," ventured Graham cautiously, "are you sure you didn't shut Alphonse into the sitting room last night? It would be easy to do."

Mrs. Norman sank down on to the bottom step of the stairs and put her head in her hands in mock despair.

"Sometimes I think I'm the only one in this house with any kind of a brain," she said. "When I shut up all the doors last night, I made absolutely sure that Alphonse was out here, in the hall. He was lying in his bed under the stairs. I'd be willing to swear to it in a court of law, if necessary," she finished dramatically.

Mr. Norman and his son exchanged a look that said, "She's imagining things" and went into the kitchen, where an odd scene met their eyes.

In front of the cooker was a bowl, a spoon, a packet of cereal and a jug of milk. They were carefully positioned as if on a table—but they were on the floor.

"Does this look like something a dog could do? asked Mrs. Norman. "In any case, I fail to see how Alphonse could have been simultaneously sleeping behind a closed door in the sitting room and helping himself to breakfast behind a closed door in the kitchen."

It was a good point.

"Well," said Graham, logic leading him to an unpleasant conclusion, "if it wasn't you, Dad, and it wasn't you, Mum, and it wasn't me, then it must have been…"

"Burglars!" screamed Mrs. Norman. "Oh my goodness, we'll all be murdered in our beds!"

"No, no, my dear. The burglar, if he was here, is gone, and we're all safe," said Mr. Norman soothingly. "We must phone the police."

It was the right thing to do, but still Mr. Norman spent an embarrassing ten minutes trying to explain to a sergeant on the other end of the phone that he was ringing to complain that there was a dog on his sofa and cereal on his kitchen floor.

No, he agreed, nothing had been stolen as far as they could see. No, there was no sign of a forced entry. What was he complaining about? Well, someone had been in his

house, without permission, and in the middle of the night. Wasn't that something to complain about?

The sergeant advised Mr. Norman to be extra careful to lock all his doors and windows that night and not to hesitate to call if anything further happened. In the meantime, it sounded as though he had had a lucky escape but there was little that the police could do."

Mr. Norman, muttering about taxpayers' money, put the phone down and helped his wife to clear up the kitchen and clear out the dog. It was typical, he thought, of Alphonse to have slept through the arrival of a burglar and not made a sound. If Graham wasn't so fond of him...

The following evening, all three members of the Norman family helped to lock up the house. It was like the launching of a space mission.

"Back door locked?"

"Check!"

"Front door locked?"

"Check!"

"Windows secure?"

"Check! Check! Check!"

"Dog shut in hall?"

"Check! Woof!"

"Everyone ready to go upstairs?"

"Check! Goodnight! Goodnight! Goodnight!"

The next morning, three figures in dressing gowns gathered on the landing and synchronized their watches.

"After you," said Mr. Norman politely to his wife.

The family crept downstairs. Alphonse was still asleep under the stairs. The doors of the hallway were all firmly closed. They looked into the kitchen. Everything seemed fine. With growing confidence, Graham strode over to the sitting room door and flung it open. There in the middle of the carpet was a strange edifice. Five cushions were piled one on top of the other. Then there was a vase. On top of that, a book was precariously balanced.

"What on earth…?" Mr. Norman took a step on to the carpet. His tread was not light at the best of times. Now, it had the same result as a sudden small earth

tremor. The balanced book crashed to the floor. The vase and the cushions followed it. None of this would have mattered so much if the vase had not turned out to be full to the brim with orange juice. A sticky mess oozed out over the beige carpet.

The Norman family held a council of war in the kitchen.

"I know it's weird, but we can't call the police," said Mr. Norman, still smarting from his last encounter with the local station. I know just how the conversation will go. 'Was anything stolen?' No. 'Was any damage done?' Well, only by me. 'Were the locks forced or the windows broken?'

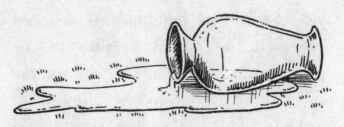

No. I cannot," Mr. Norman went on, "ask the police to come and investigate a pile of cushions. You must see that."

Sadly, Mrs. Norman did see that. But she was badly shaken.

"Do you know what I'm thinking?" she hissed. "Poltergeists! Horrible ghostly things that throw stuff around. We've got one! I can feel it!"

"It's got a very odd sense of humour," said Mr. Norman. "I never liked those cushions, you know."

"They were *beautiful*!"

Mrs. Norman felt inclined to make another theatrical gesture. Sometimes she felt it was high time she returned to the stage. Sometimes her husband and son thought so, too.

"There is only one thing we can do," said Graham, practically. "We either have a particularly bungling burglar, who seems unable to grasp the fact that he's supposed to steal something while he's in here, or we have some other kind of ... er ... manifestation. The only way we can find out is to watch and catch him in the act. We can take it in turns tonight."

It was a good plan, but Mrs. Norman declared that her nerves were in shreds and quite unequal to the task. Mr. Norman declared that once he was asleep he was dead to the world and quite impossible to

wake. Not for the first time, Graham decided that the task was his alone.

Late that night, after giving Alf full instructions about how to behave, Graham went up to bed as usual. When he heard his parents come up, he waited half an hour. Then he silently slipped out of his room and downstairs, reminding Alf to be quiet in a stage whisper his mother would have been proud of.

Under the stairs, Graham shared Alf's basket. The hours passed slowly and it was terribly tempting to go to sleep, but Graham kept reminding himself that he was upholding the honour of Alf, who was still strangely under suspicion although it was obvious that he could have had a paw in none of the odd occurrences.

At half past two, Graham heard a creaking sound. He stiffened, grasping his torch more tightly, and waited. He was

pretty sure that poltergeists didn't creak, whatever else they did.

As the creaking grew louder and louder, Graham could bear the waiting no longer. He jumped out of his hiding place and shone the torch ... straight into the blank face of his sleepwalking father. As he watched, Mr. Norman walked calmly to a pot-plant he particularly loathed and began to pluck the leaves from it.

Graham rapidly considered his options. What was more likely to bring about family harmony? A suspected poltergeist or a proved ornament-smashing and pot-plant pillaging father? It was not a difficult decision. Gently, Graham led his father back to bed and went back downstairs to find the encyclopedia. He decided he needed to know a lot more about poltergeists, now that he knew they had one.